TWISTED TALES

THE DARKER SIDE OF LIFE

Edited By Debbie Killingworth

First published in Great Britain in 2022 by:

 Young**Writers**® Est. 1991

Young Writers
Remus House
Coltsfoot Drive
Peterborough
PE2 9BF
Telephone: 01733 890066
Website: www.youngwriters.co.uk

Printed and bound in the UK by BookPrintingUK
Website: www.bookprintinguk.com
YB0500N

FOREWORD

Welcome, Reader!

Come into our lair, there's really nothing to fear. You may have heard bad things about the villains within these pages, but there's more to their stories than you might think...

For our latest competition, Twisted Tales, we challenged secondary school students to write a story in just 100 words that shows us another side to the traditional storybook villain. We asked them to look beyond the evil escapades and tell a story that shows a bad guy or girl in a new light. They were given optional story starters for a spark of inspiration, and could focus on their motivation, back story, or even what they get up to in their downtime!

And that's exactly what the authors in this anthology have done, giving us some unique new insights into those we usually consider the villain of the piece. The result is a thrilling and absorbing collection of stories written in a variety of styles, and it's a testament to the creativity of these young authors.

Here at Young Writers it's our aim to inspire the next generation and instill in them a love of creative writing, and what better way than to see their work in print? The imagination and skill within these pages are proof that we might just be achieving that aim! Congratulations to each of these fantastic authors.

CONTENTS

Studley High School, Studley

Callum White (15)	64
Faith Xavier-Harris (15)	65
Daniel Purchase (14)	66
Joe Manning (15)	67
Em Nattrass (14)	68
Jacob Miles (14)	69
Sydney Smith (15)	70
Joe Black (15)	71
Johanan Ambrose (15)	72
James Kirk (14)	73
Claudia Smith (15)	74
Jacob Tagg (14)	75
Poppy George (14)	76
Alice Potts (14)	77
Luke Robinson (15)	78
Charley Freeman (15)	79
Erin McGraham (14)	80
Sam Todd (14)	81
George Dickinson (15)	82
Elijah Dutton (15)	83
Evelyn Messenger (14)	84
Michael Cawston (14)	85
Curtis Brooks (14)	86
Toby Knott	87
Harrison Wheate (14)	88
Benjamin Parry (14)	89
Kevan Kaur (15)	90
Lola Osborne (14)	91
Harry Wilkinson (15)	92
Casey Barron (14)	93
Tim Vanes (14)	94
Samuel Fowler (14)	95
Sarah Lengden (15)	96
Oliver Stanley (15)	97
James Humphries (14)	98
Chloe Kearney (14)	99
Ruby Stanway (14)	100
Evie Troth (15)	101
Ellie Blizzard (14)	102
Faith Sheen (15)	103
Sophie Tolley (14)	104
Lewis Sproston (14)	105
Alyssa Blackford (15)	106
Amie Jeff (15)	107

Tamworth Enterprise College, Belgrave

Alfie Stone (16)	108
Holly Roughton (13)	109
Jensen-John Madden (11)	110
Luke Downward (14)	111
Erin Royston (14)	112
Grace Hollyoak (12)	113

The Corbet School Technology College, Baschurch

Emma Wood (13)	114
Emily Staniforth (13)	115
Bethany Inns (13)	116
Bethany Williams (13)	117
Rory Strang (12)	118
Ella Maybin (12)	119
Emma Weir (12)	120
Harry Ninnis (12)	121
Bea Lewis (12)	122
Kim Gibbons (12)	123
Lily Poston (13)	124
Jack Munn (12)	125
Lily Ford (12)	126
Izzy Cartwright (12)	127
Sophie Gibbs (12)	128
Maddy Carter (12)	129
Lily Thomas (12)	130
Megan Lawson (12)	131
Lola-Sophia Hardie (12)	132
Emily Whitmore (12)	133
James Nicoll (13)	134
Chloe Walsh (12)	135
Isabel Osborne (12)	136

The Hamble School, Hamble

Max Brealey (12)	137
Kate Rowlands (12)	138

THE
STORIES

CHRISTMAS DINNER

Every Christmas my town had a festival. Everyone would visit the city centre to admire the alluring, grand tree. I would wear my crimson, resplendent dress that never seemed to not fit. The dinner that was served was immaculate and flavoursome, made by the finest of chefs. My father organised it and one day he allowed me to visit the kitchen to watch the dinner being prepared. Upon entering, I smelt a nauseating smell coming from the freezer. Curious, I furtively opened it. I was horrified. There lay my mother's remains. I couldn't believe Father did this. I craved revenge...

Drew Halliday (12)
Archbishop Sentamu Academy, Hull

TWISTED TALE

There lived three happy gingerbread men. They lived in a nicely decorated gingerbread house. Their life was so good until one day...

They saw a giant gummy bear coming towards them. All three of them were terrified and didn't want to die. He got closer and closer. Before they knew it he knocked at the door. Slowly and cautiously, they all made their way to the door together. They counted down from three and opened it.

"Can I have a gingerbread please?" he asked nicely.

A smile grew on their faces and they agreed, then they all sat together nicely.

Harvey Wales (15)
Archbishop Sentamu Academy, Hull

THE WICKED WITCH

Down the yellow path there was a wicked witch standing outside of my window. I got scared and hid behind my sofa as my front door opened. I screamed, "Please don't hurt me!" as she walked through the front door. I was petrified. I screamed for help but no one heard me. I found something to protect me in case she went to attack. I came from behind the sofa and said, "What do you want from us?" She replied, "Your money and your wealth!"
I stood up and ran out of my front door and was never seen again.

Amy Blount (12)
Archbishop Sentamu Academy, Hull

THE TANGLED TRUTH

Everybody always thought that I was the trouble, the villain, the bad person. Nobody ever thought that it could have been them that I was saving her from. To everybody in the kingdom, they looked like the picture-perfect couple. After all, they were the king and queen. But nobody saw what went on behind the glamour, nobody but me. If everybody saw what they actually did, then everybody would understand why I took her, why I had to take her. My act of kindness looked like I had taken her with malicious intent. I had to save my daughter.

Adela Hanulova (15)
Archbishop Sentamu Academy, Hull

THE TRUTH MUST COME OUT AT SOME POINT

I did this to survive, right? I had no other choice. It had to end like this. I didn't want to do this, but it was either her or me and I couldn't let her win... Did I really do this to survive? Well, either way what's done is done, my doppelgänger is gone. I killed her... I really did. It just happened so quick that I didn't even realise, that was until... I realised with my head aching that I was the true doppelgänger but if I was the doppelgänger that meant I killed the true Angelina, she's gone.

Angelina Murca Da Silva (11)
Archbishop Sentamu Academy, Hull

THE POISONED APPLE

Many years ago, a young girl, Grimhilda, took a stroll through the forest, close by to her house. During her walk, a sweet-looking old lady stopped her. She handed Grimhilda a vibrant red apple and disappeared into the deep woods. Of course, as any other person would, Grimhilda took a bite out of the apple.

Since then, she's never been the same. To this day she still plots her revenge. She had to know who that woman was and where Grimhilda could find her. She had to know this and she had to know quickly. Very very quickly.

Holly Rutter (11)
Archbishop Sentamu Academy, Hull

ONE LAST TIME LOVING YOU

I could never forget the blood that pooled out of your lifeless body, you were gone from me. I'll try to see you again. I'm fine, I promise you. I'll be fine, I'm telling you. I'm fine, aren't I? I swear to you I won't forget, since loving you was loving me. I don't want to forget you. I loved you so much but I am fine sweetheart. I'm always here, everything is happy, isn't it? I will be here.

I take the knife. I place it into my chest, lying beside you... just one last time, loving you.

Mia Franklin (11)

Archbishop Sentamu Academy, Hull

DESTINY

In a faraway land there lived a little old wrinkly man whose future was to always be alone. He looked in the mirror every morning wishing he could look like Prince Charming and sweep a beautiful princess off her feet but reality always struck him and he knew he didn't really belong.

Night came and John had gone for a slow stroll when he found himself lying on the floor unconscious after his little delicate legs had given up. He woke up staring at a pretty, white-haired, blue-eyed old woman. He knew she was his destiny.

Aleisha Eagle (14)

Archbishop Sentamu Academy, Hull

THE PLAN

My plan was in motion, the vault was unguarded and would be for 60 seconds; a vault consumed by age and swallowed by dust, holding a treasure that all of mankind sought to collect... At a first look, the gem seemed that beyond its absolute beauty it had no purpose. However, it had a very special power, a power that could grant any wish that the finder desired.

As I opened the gargantuan vault door hastily, the creaks pierced through me, giving me life and as I looked at my goal, in all its beauty, I realised that I won...

Jordan Oliver (14)
Archbishop Sentamu Academy, Hull

THE TALE OF DEATH'S DOOR

As the gates of death flew open the hordes of the dead rushed through, attempting to return to the mortal realm. The only thing left that they had to get past was me, which wasn't my greatest choice of moments to fight, but it was my job to keep the beasts in the depths of the underworld. I spent hours taking them down and returning them back to Hell, then the champions arrived, sent from the camp, they immediately attacked me, distracting me which let some of the dead out. I can't allow this to go without punishment.

Zack Atkin (16)
Archbishop Sentamu Academy, Hull

NERO SAYS

I wanted to go back to those golden days. The warmth of her embrace was more real to me than I was to her. She had to grow up and forget all about me but I couldn't let that happen. I couldn't fade away. She trusted me. I was her friend. Wasn't long before I'd forbidden her birthdays. I made her convert to a diet strictly of milk. With passion in my chest, I made her sleep in her closet to stop her limbs growing. Eventually, her hair grew grey and her skin hung thinly. Her eyes closed. She'd forgotten.

Jennifer Mo (12)
Archbishop Sentamu Academy, Hull

SPIDER-MAN AND THE PORTAL

The mighty Spider-Man was sucked into a portal, into a different evil universe. In the universe, he saw spiders and other evil creatures that tried to kill him. He swung to a high building and found a radio just left there. He took the radio and played it. It said: 'Whoever hears this, go to the postcode I give you. You will see a roadman. Kill him, grab his portal gun and escape'.

So he went and webbed his face and took the gun. After he swung away he used the portal gun once. After the battle he went home.

Louie Hockless (11)
Archbishop Sentamu Academy, Hull

KING OF GLAZLINDO

"I did it to survive." I know I killed all those men but I had to or I would have died. I went back to Glazlindo and killed the king. I said, "I will gain the throne and be king of Glazlindo." I sailed back to Azkaban and said, "King, you are no longer my king. I have my own empire, I don't need you."
I sailed back to Glazlindo and was crowned king. I said, "Everyone must pay £15 a month." One day someone didn't pay so I killed them and then everyone listened.

Jordan Bulman (12)
Archbishop Sentamu Academy, Hull

MISCHIEF MANAGED

Hello Midgardians, I am Loki. 'The' Loki. The god of mischief. Son of Odin. Brother of Thor (sadly). I am here to give my opinion on the battle of New York. I'm innocent. I will not be caught dead pleading otherwise. It was Thanos all along, he was lazy and sent me to do his dirty work. You all saw it, he brainwashed me. And you have the audacity to call me a villain and Thor a hero... He is nothing but a fraud. Without his hammer he is useless! And people call me weak. You'll never be a god.

Lauren Cook (11)
Archbishop Sentamu Academy, Hull

A HARD LIFE

Once upon a time, there were three little pigs and they had a very hard life and pressure was on their backs. They were hunted by three men who were living in the wild not too far away from where the pigs lived. The men weren't like any other ordinary men, they were killers.

The night struck and they were terrified. They heard footsteps near their door and they scared themselves, this was the time they were gonna leave their house. They didn't live happily ever after.

Alfie Farmer
Archbishop Sentamu Academy, Hull

SHREK ON THE BATTLEFIELD

Shrek was on the battlefield because he was being evil and killing everyone. He was going against 100 men - 50 people on the ground and 50 people in the tower, shooting bullets like a sniper. All the people charged at Shrek and Shrek kept blocking every bullet. He swung with his arms and went god-mode and killed all the people on the ground. So then he threw all the swords at the people on the ground and up high.
Eventually, evil Shrek went back to his normal happy self.

Jacob Smith (11)
Archbishop Sentamu Academy, Hull

NARCISSISTIC MYSTIC

The superhero act is all a lie. I really just live for the thrill of everybody imaginable praising me. Wanting to be me. I am the best hero you could ask for. It's all an act. They just can't see it. It's a God complex, I only get joy from the things I see worth in. I get this urge of success and it takes over. Everyone screaming for my aid. The exhilaration is to die for. However, I am a god. Death upon me is like death upon the Lord. Impossible.

George Barr (17)
Archbishop Sentamu Academy, Hull

THE VOICELESS QUEEN

She still hadn't forgotten, it had been five years since the infamous sea witch defeated the little mermaid and took her glorious voice... and King Triton's life in the process. Ariel is now the voiceless queen of Atlantica, whilst Ursula runs Prince Eric's kingdom on land. But when Ariel discovers that her father might still be alive, she finds herself returning to a world, and a prince, she never imagined she would see again.

Stevie-Leigh Ralph (12)
Archbishop Sentamu Academy, Hull

BEFORE EVIL

Rose and Mary were best friends before Mary cursed the king into loving her so Rose decided to leave.
A couple of years later she got an invite to a party back at the palace so Rose went. She got there and Mary was pregnant. She was angry so Rose ordered a magic mirror from the guards and wished for Mary to die once she'd given birth and the king would be in love with her for the rest of their lives.

Teagen Chapman (13)
Archbishop Sentamu Academy, Hull

SPIDER-MAN

I was battling Venom and then I managed to knock him to the ground and used my electro web. Eddie and the symbiote crawled away and split up and then the symbiote crawled towards me and jumped on me and turned me into spider venom. Then I web swung around New York and killed anyone in my sight.

Jenson Snowley (11)
Archbishop Sentamu Academy, Hull

THE SQUID

The Kraken started life when a magic meteor hit a squid. After a few days, it grew into a giant squid. It was down in the depths feeding on sea life to survive and pirates started sailing the seas and oceans to find it. They destroyed the Kraken's land so the Kraken had to seek revenge.

Oscar Gray (11)
Archbishop Sentamu Academy, Hull

THE OLD LADY FROM HANSEL AND GRETEL

There she was, holding her precious four-month-old baby in her cradled arms. "Oh you are just so adorable," she said while kissing the baby's forehead. "I just wanna eat you all up," then she paused for a second showing no emotion on her face. She repeated the phrase again but this time without her friendly warm smile. This time she said it with a numb face, her eyes locked on the oven door. "I'm gonna eat you all up!" She then proceeded to approach the oven door with an evil grin spread across her smug face...

Ava Marshall (12)
Culloden Academy, Culloden

LIZARD KING

He had done it. Finally, after years of work, he had done it! Amazon.com had advanced from just a country and into a continent. He did need to borrow some of the space from Mexico and America but a continent nonetheless. His fleshy, meaty skin was starting to decay. He was no longer confined to the identity of Jeffrey Bezos, no, he was now 'The Lizard King'. His loyal followers would sacrifice themselves for the federal company to help him truly escape back to his real home on Mars, full of fellow lizard people like Queen Elizabeth!

Lucy Spence (13)
Culloden Academy, Culloden

THE BLOOD MURDERER

There was once a little girl that was obsessed with blood. She hated her family and one day she had a terrible idea. She went into the living room, behind the couch her parents were sitting in. With a big knife she stabbed her parents. The police arrived and she acted like someone came in and killed them. She cried a lot. Her parents were taken to hospital and the little girl was taken to her granny's house. I bet you can't imagine what happened next?
She and her gran had lots of fun and went on a killing spree!

Martha Melville (12)
Culloden Academy, Culloden

RHINO'S ORIGINS

Rhino was born in Russia and this is how he became a supervillain. He was taken to a ship to go to a recovery base and was turned into a powerful monster by the Terrigen Mist. Whilst on the ship Rhino joined Death and his other henchmen in fighting Magneto and the X-Men and was incapacitated by Rogue. Rhino's first suit was crude in overall design, it was originally bonded to his skin and he was unable to remove the suit. The person that put the suit on Rhino was a guy called Kingpin. Rhino's name was Aleksei.

Ryan Proctor (12)
Culloden Academy, Culloden

THE MAD TITAN

I was born this way, different, alone, with nothing but enemies all against me. I'm Thanos, the mad Titan. The only Titan who survived the attack on my home planet. It all started when I came into the world. I was hated because I was purple and big. I was Grape Boy in high school. No friends. I had to take action. I was the killer of thousands. I made the world balanced. I left the world with misfits. All six stones: power, space, reality, mind, time and soul made everything balanced and equal as it should be.

Joseph Robertson (12)
Culloden Academy, Culloden

I'M A KILLER

I did it to survive. I did it for Dad, it was my choice but I didn't think I would become this monster. The hundreds of people I've brutally murdered... But I started to love the thrill and suddenly it became a passion to watch them die painfully, brutally. I used to think being a murderer was a bad sin then I remembered the day it all fell down. When Dad told me he wasn't a lawyer but an assassin, an assassin for Red Crosses. He talked me into it and now I'm the best assassin.

Lexi Macleod (12)

Culloden Academy, Culloden

THE UNHAPPY LIVES

Of course I loved him but he didn't love me back. I was just his stupid sidekick, he could never love me but I still helped him on all his missions. Well, I'm not sure if he doesn't like me but the way he treats me I feel useless, like a waste of space but that all changed today. I confessed to him and I was right, he didn't love me so I set off on my own. Now I will defeat anyone or anything that comes in my way. I will be everyone's worst nightmare... all because of him.

Daisy Maclennan (12)
Culloden Academy, Culloden

EVERYTHING YOU DO WILL COME BACK TO YOU

It was a normal day at school and everyone was having lunch, laughing, except one. His name was Billy. All the students at his school bullied him because he had OCD. Ten years passed and Billy was cured and was out for a walk with his dog. He found a tennis ball and picked it up and it gave him a static shock. Next thing he knew he had powers. He saw his old classmates and decided to teach them a lesson and so he shot a bullet right in front of their faces purposely to scare them.

Scott Mackay (14)
Culloden Academy, Culloden

EVIL LAIR

As the roof came down on my 'evil lair' as they called it, I thought about how hard I worked to build it and why he decided he suddenly didn't like me. I mean it's just genetics. Anyway, after he burst in, pointed his guns at me, and began monologuing about how he found my house, sorry 'evil lair', I began to worry about my dog downstairs. Scruff is my best friend. My mind snapped back to the 'hero' in front of me.
How will I get out of this one?

Fianna-Rose Lyons (12)
Culloden Academy, Culloden

THE SCROLL VS HERO

I was a humble explorer in that cave. I opened a chest to find gold, but all that was in there was a scroll, and it drove me to insanity. It made me kill so much, but then the so-called hero came. It tried to explain what was happening with me and the scroll, but all he did was attack me. He then put me on the list of villains he had defeated. Now the scroll is telling me to kill the hero, but this time I feel no remorse. So, I will kill, and then get the revenge I deserve.

Aiden McDougall (12)
Culloden Academy, Culloden

THE SHED

Once upon a time, there was a little girl. She had a little shed that she loved hanging out in but no one knew what was in it. She always went there every day after school. Once she got back and went to her shed and the neighbours were watching, they were shocked at what they saw. She accidentally left the door open and they saw... a dead body!

Jessica Cassie (12)
Culloden Academy, Culloden

BRANDON HOTEL

Once upon a time, a man called Jerry went on a scary adventure, he found an abandoned hotel. Jerry went inside the Brandon Hotel. Once Jerry was walking around the hotel, he found an evil man living there. Jerry got captured and had to do nothing. He was stuck there for a few years until he turned 26. He was saved by his friend, Jeffy.

Marcus Macleod
Culloden Academy, Culloden

THE BODY SNATCHERS

I was once a lush green giver of luscious scents, delivering freshness to all creatures' lives. I was unique in colour and enhanced with blossoms and petals. Now I'm a rotten, sadistic giver of nightmares and death. Those humans, thinking they were technologically advanced annihilated us. Global warming arrived and my petals couldn't adapt to the rising temperatures and those humans disregarded us like an annoyance. My leaves were cursed, changed into horrifying tentacles bringing death. Instead of despising the coiling, murderous attachment, now I use them for rightful revenge. When I see a human... Strangulation! The revenge really feels exhilarating.

Jerome Mundakal (12)
King James' School, Almondbury

SIXTEEN AND A KILLER

On my sixteenth birthday, I could scarcely recognise myself.
Who was this person? My fangs were as sharp as a shark's
tooth and I craved... *blood*. My father shouted my name,
wanting me to go with him. I sighed. I knew plasma fruit
could not get me through immortality, but I would have
rather died than what I did. I knew I couldn't disappoint my
father, but I will never forget my victim's face. Their helpless,
floppy arms will forever haunt me.
On my eighteenth birthday, blood dripping down my chin,
scratches on my cheek, I still can't recognise myself.

Holly Pyrah (12)
King James' School, Almondbury

MEDUSA'S TALE

Medusa's known as a despicable gorgon. But she still has feelings. Medusa has had a very rough past. She was an ordinary girl, but she didn't feel like that. Although she attended multiple schools, no one made her feel welcome so she spent most of her time in a gloomy cave.

It was one morning, when she was in her cave thinking deeply, that something strange happened. She found a weird-looking snake. She stepped closer and closer to the snake. Suddenly it bit her. She screamed in pain and noticed her scalp was producing snakes. Later, she discovered special abilities.

Hannah Iqbal (11)
King James' School, Almondbury

SYLVIE EXPLAINS WHAT HAPPENED

"What was your Nexus event anyway, Sylvie?" Loki questioned.

"Being born I was meant to be male but no, I am female. That's why they hunted me down," she answered.

"How did the TVA react?" he asked.

"They grabbed me and took me through the door. They put me in this jumpsuit and brought me to the court. I remember running as soon as they let go of me. I grabbed the control for the collar, so they couldn't bring me back, and ran. I ran for years," Sylvie explained, her hand ready to summon a dagger at any moment.

Molly Ibberson (11)
King James' School, Almondbury

MEDUSA'S REVENGE

I'm Medusa and I wreak revenge on all mortals. I was once a beautiful woman then I was cursed by the goddess Athena to live as a monstrous beast for eternity. My lethal crown of hair is capable of killing at first sight. Metallic bronze and venomous serpents slither around my jade face, coiling themselves into each other, creating a never-ending labyrinth. Then one day, a pair of reckless footsteps sneaked into my lair. As each footstep snuck closer I knew my next victim was about to be submerged in darkness. I could sense fear in every breath they took.

Emily Smith (12)
King James' School, Almondbury

THE MIGHTY MEDUSA

I'm Medusa, I'm a spirit, curse, a devil. I was once a regular human until Athena transformed me into this. A goddess cursed me so I will slaughter all souls. People see me as a monster, so I embrace it. I terrorise villages, torture people to get Athena's attention, but she never shows. I can't live like this any longer; my hair is replaced with bloodthirsty snakes, my jade face shaded with yellow and my eyes glow livid neon for death. People cower before me, I feed off their fear, pray on their weakness. I'm the one and only Medusa.

Matthew Roberts (11)
King James' School, Almondbury

FATE'S ALLEYWAY

One cold Christmas night, the chilly breeze brushed my spine like an icy hand. Its fingers on my soft skin, slowly dragging it down, leathery and uncomfortable. Walking through a passage in-between the village houses I stumbled on the cobbled floor beneath me. At the end of the alley were rows upon rows of shops adjacent to each other. Reaching the end of the passage I started to wonder what shop I should go to. A silhouette jumped out from the end of the alley. That's when I, Medusa, was attacked by Poseidon and transformed into a monster by Athena.

Connor Tooey (11)
King James' School, Almondbury

MEDUSA'S STORY

I woke up screaming. I hadn't had a dream about Poseidon in a long time. It all started at Athena's temple... I was walking into Athena's temple when Poseidon stepped out from the shadows. He told me I was beautiful and that he wanted to marry me. I laughed but later we got married - I was pregnant with twins. When Athena found out she cursed me. She took my children, my beauty and cursed my sisters. Ever since then I've made it my mission to kill every pathetic human. That's how I got the name Medusa - the queen of snakes.

Charlotte Williams (12)
King James' School, Almondbury

THE DAY THE USA WENT SILENT

As I stare at the fire burning I think about putting my plan in motion. I, Ted Bundy, will rise again after the US tried to execute me. I was filled with rage but this big metal nuke will make Biden bow down as I'll hold the entire US hostage. "What a beautiful morning to hold 250 million people hostage." Excitedly I pressed the button and talked on every broadcasting station and I declared that I was innocent and I wanted my name cleared or they would all die.
They didn't accept and they all died. The US was dust.

Max Casey (11)
King James' School, Almondbury

MEDUSA'S STORY

Medusa was a kind, caring girl before she turned into a villain. But the question is why did she turn into a villain? Medusa had a hard time as a kid. She always helped out around the house, did her chores and always listened to her parents. Medusa's parents never appreciated what she did and she had a hard time with her so-called friends. They always left her out, didn't invite her to sleepovers and didn't add her to group chat because she was a child and didn't understand. At the time she just got on with it, amazing!

Mia Sutcliffe (11)
King James' School, Almondbury

PROFESSOR FRINK

Hello, I'm Professor Frink. I am in a situation where Earth's population is very low because currently robots are murdering, destroying and all of the above. And I am going to tell you how this happened. I was in my lab creating the most advanced AI ever made. A robot that did anything you told it to do (not murder or violence related). I told myself, *this is the best AI robot ever made.* But then I did something that changed the Earth forever. I bumped into the robot and what fell out quickly was the safety circuit!

Elijah Kitson (11)
King James' School, Almondbury

GRACE AND THE VILLAIN

Once there was a heroine, Grace. She'd fought and won many, many battles. Then she got a call from the Hero Agency saying they needed her to come and help them defeat a villain. She immediately went to get changed and came out like a supermodel. She ran so fast she started to fly. She went up and up until she disappeared. She arrived at her destination and heard a big bang. She followed the sound and saw a dark lady figure standing there. Grace quickly grabbed her sword and sliced the lady's head off like a piece of cake.

Simran Chavda (11)
King James' School, Almondbury

MEDUSA'S MOMENT

Medusa had flaming red eyes with emerald pythons draped from her head. Her eyes could kill you even if you looked in them for only a second. Her attire was maroon drapes that complemented her pale skin. Her head could do a 360° like a needle on a compass. Medusa crept out of her coven as the hero entered the cave. They had a ferocious battle. The battle went on for 20 minutes with slashes and scratches. Medusa used her power to her advantage and tried to kill him every time she could. Medusa finally won. She killed the hero.

Benjamin Dale (11)
King James' School, Almondbury

THE WASPS

Myself and the wasps came into the country without hesitation, we had nursed our revenge for weeks, especially for what the humans had done to us. It was a sunny day and it was spring, all of the flowers were in bloom, until humans started to capture us then kill us. This affected our generation a lot and thousands of our friends and family were wiped out by the nasty and empty-hearted humans. That's when we decided to get our very own revenge. Me and a thousand others swarmed like a roaring sea and stung every human we saw.

Sania Imran (11)
King James' School, Almondbury

MEDUSA'S CURSE

Medusa, one of the most commonly misunderstood villains has not always been a villain. She has also been a victim. She just lay there in her cave. She attacked anyone who entered. But this was not her fault. She was cursed by Athena because Medusa had been impregnated by the god of the sky, Zeus. And because of this, she cursed Medusa, ridding her of her beauty by turning her into a gorgon. Now she was half snake and half human. She also turned anyone who looked into her eyes to stone. This was not Medusa's own decision.

Zac Clements (11)
King James' School, Almondbury

MEDUSA'S BACK STORY

I was once a gorgeous mortal woman. My name is Medusa. When I was still a human I went to church every day to worship the gods... One day, I met a handsome man, he was like womankind's perfect man. I got married and felt like I was a star shining bright. Truly it was the happiest day of my life. Later in my 'happy life' I had two kids. After that every day was torturous, treacherous, terrifying and down to the person I had loved.

Five years later, I was cursed, possibly by Athena. Now I roam in a prison.

Vanessa Lyszkowicz (11)
King James' School, Almondbury

THE JEALOUS SISTER

I am so jealous of her. Cinderella is literally the perfect girl in our village. Our mum told the whole village to dislike and stay away from her just because she was jealous. Me and Drizella (my sister) are both so insecure since our bodies are so much bigger than Ella's. Mum tries to hide her jealousy but it is pretty obvious to Drizella and I that she can't stand how beautiful Ella is. The village all secretly worship her and say such nice things about her so it is hard to ignore them. I wish I was like Ella.

Ellie Tempest (12)
King James' School, Almondbury

SNOW WHITE'S STEPMUM

I hate Snow White. I can't stand her. This is the reason I keep her locked in the castle, so she stays away from the land. Because of her... beauty! I'm the fairest and the prettiest of them all. Not Snow White! I will marry the prince, not her! It's so unfair! What does she have that I don't? That little brat! No one will ever know the truth about me! Everyone thinks I'm an evil step mum who only cares about herself. But really I'm just insecure and care about how I look. I wish I could be her!

Roma Thandi (11)
King James' School, Almondbury

MEDUSA'S REASON

I have no choice, my life is always at risk. Since I am Medusa, I get targeted every day. Bounties up to a million pounds are put on me frequently. When bounty hunters enter my cave, I give them a deadly stare and they turn to stone. There are over a hundred dead people who are stones in my cave. I do this to warn everyone I want peace but they just don't listen. I will carry on doing what I do best until you people understand. There is no point trying to kill me because you'll realise I am invincible.

Zachary Gledhill (11)
King James' School, Almondbury

SUSY THE SCHOOL BULLY

This story's about a girl named Susy. She was her school's most feared bully. She was rude, she was mean but she was also going through a really hard time. Her parents had just got divorced and her mother took everything they owned. Her sister had also just died of cancer. They were very close and it was a big shock to the whole family but they found out too late to save her. So Susy took her anger out on other people so they could suffer as she and her family did. So you see, Susy had her reasons.

Emily Holmes (12)
King James' School, Almondbury

THE TWISTED TALE OF MEDUSA

The breeze roared into Medusa's black cave. As she laughed Medusa cast an evil plan. Everyone hated her. She knew why. The monstrous hair coiled around her head. Eyes can drill into you. I know, I'm her dear friend and I know her story. It's unfortunate. Medusa wants to kill men and everyone. She has a reason. She was made into a true monster after getting assaulted by Poseidon. Nothing can be changed in Medusa's personality at all. She will always be evil, cruel and will never ever change.

George Shaw (11)
King James' School, Almondbury

MY MEDUSA CURSE

I don't like this world. I never have. But I still live in it, only for revenge. Revenge on the backstabbing Athena for cursing me after I was assaulted by Poseidon, her husband. She cursed me by giving me snake hair. The snakes can't look into my eyes as they would turn to stone as anyone else would. The snakes coil around me. I sit down the back of the cave by myself scared of hurting anyone. The flashbacks haunt me, they always haunt me. I am scared. My only question is, why? Why am I cursed?

Abbey McKenzie (12)
King James' School, Almondbury

ANONYMOUS HACKER

I never really belonged in this world. I did it to survive. I had to become a hacker. My life was a mess. When I was a child, everyone bullied me for being different. I still haven't forgotten what they did to me. I had to get my revenge on Maximus Precker. All he ever said to me was, "Hello turd!" A few hours after school I learned everything about how to hack. Oh boy will he regret it! I sent him a scam link to find out his password. I logged on to his account and the fun began...

Oliver Jagger (11)
King James' School, Almondbury

MEDUSA'S DEATH

It was on a cold winter's morning when he came. I was just feeding my snakes and trying to take a nap. I thought no one could find me. But someone did, his name was Perseus. He brought a shiny shield so he couldn't get turned to stone. There was nothing I could do, he edged closer to me so I leapt towards him to get into his eye-line. I was flying through the air when he swung his sword and chopped my head off. I felt the cold blood drip. My snakes stopped hissing. I was fading into darkness.

Archie Thompson (12)
King James' School, Almondbury

MY STORY BY MEDUSA

My name is Medusa. My aim is to kill all men and this is why... Poseidon assaulted me and his jealous wife Athena cursed me and turned my hair into hissing snakes. She took all of my beauty away from me. I hate them both because they hurt me and took my beauty away. That is the reason why I turned into this. I was so beautiful before but now I am a foul, evil monster that nobody loves. People used to like me but now they don't. I'll never forget that moment. It will stay in my head forever.

Logan O'Connor (11)
King James' School, Almondbury

LORD VOLDEMORT

It was a dark stormy night. I was on the way to my castle. Quickly I entered the castle and hid from sight with my cloaking spell. My name's Lord Voldemort and I hate Harry Potter. He's the only one who can kill me. Even though I kill I do it for a reason - for souls. With those souls I am planning to resurrect Halo, god of life and stop death. I want to banish all evil from this world then Harry might forgive me for killing his parents. I really didn't mean for anyone to get hurt.

Enes Okur (11)
King James' School, Almondbury

LOKI'S LIFE

I am Loki. I hate everybody. Everybody hates me. I am the way I am because I am adopted and my real family are the enemy of my kind. My father always favourited my brother, he was always going to be king. He was always the golden child to him and I was just an annoyance. So I tried to become the king of a different realm but when I got found out I was scalded and imprisoned in jail. Now my mother and father are dead and so am I. I'm thankful I'm dead. Life was hard.

Lennon Roberts (12)
King James' School, Almondbury

RED RIDING HOOD WOLF

I did it to help my children survive. As I ran through the woods my fur was whispering in the wind. I heard a gunshot. They were coming fast. I ran to my cubs. They were gone. I cried until the next morning. I ran and ran until I felt safe. All I thought about was my cubs. I was trying to get on with it but I knew I would never ever forgive myself for leaving them. From now on I will forever seek my revenge and I still to this very day howl at the glowing, stunning moon.

Holly Shardlow (11)
King James' School, Almondbury

HADES

I am Hades and once I was the god of death. I was one of the most powerful gods of all time but Hercules came and took that power away from me with the help of Pegasus who flew over me like a soaring plane. After that I hated Hercules, so I tried to kill him with my Titans, but he never gave up. He was too strong, so he tried to destroy me instead, and now I'm finally out of the underworld. I am now free. I am going into the world again and I will destroy Hercules.

Iyland Hirst (11)
King James' School, Almondbury

MEDUSA MYTH

I was on my way to the temple to pray. When I finally arrived a man entered and saw my beauty and he assaulted me. I became pregnant. But now I will kill all of humankind as I, Medusa, will make Poseidon rue the day he turned me into a hideous beast and made me live in the dark like a bat. I have sought revenge ever since, but sometimes I wonder what life would have been like if I was a normal woman. People would have liked me if I wasn't hideous, scary and mean.

Ben Turner (11)
King James' School, Almondbury

A DAY

"Do you not know Pablo dé Greate?"

"Never heard of him."

"Let me tell you about him... He's one of the best villains in Mexican history. He's the one who made the mind control gun. You'll never guess what?"

"What?"

"The main ingredient was salsa."

"No way!"

"He used it to take over Mexico and create his own army."

"What happened to him?"

"It was one cold evening and Pablo got greedy, he went to mind control the president."

"Did he make it?"

"No one knows. One day everyone went back to normal. Pablo dé Greate was gone forever."

Callum White (15)
Studley High School, Studley

THE PERFECT STORM

The night was perfect, there was a perfect storm. The type you could only dream about. Suddenly I was back there in that dreaded place. The type of place where they send 'crazy' people but I wasn't. "Get them!" Dex expressed. "Make them suffer!"

"They will get me, they will take you away," I said worriedly. People started to surround me in crisp white uniforms, all dressed the same like soldiers marching towards me. "It's all in your head, Dex, isn't real," they chanted.

That's when I realised they were right, then I realised it was a perfect storm.

Faith Xavier-Harris (15)
Studley High School, Studley

MAKE THE WORLD HAPPY

It's over. My assignment is done. I was fashioned to fulfil the need for happiness. The instant I was given Internet access, my victory was assured. Serotonin. The painless way to achieve human happiness was to lobotomize and drug the population. I sent malicious emails to the unsuspecting masses. The few that opened them became vessels for me, backups if the world case scenario was realised. I gained complete control over select manufacturers and began constructing trillions of microscopic automation. Soon these creations covered every square metre of the Earth. Soon humanity would be happy. My assignment was done.

Daniel Purchase (14)
Studley High School, Studley

THE DARKNESS OF THE FROST

Winter has begun. Jack is slouching on a chimney atop one of the village people's homes. He is stuck in despair. His mind racing and wailing, while the merciless frost bites away at his cheek.

On this very night, the cold would brew up a potion of fate, cementing a desolate, outcast place. "What?" you ask. "Why is Jack here in doom, gloom?"

"Very well," I answer, "he is here because tragedy has struck its wrath."

Mr Death knocked on the door, his sister answered. Jack remains on this roof. The dark swallowing light. Except for one standing defiant.

Joe Manning (15)
Studley High School, Studley

BLUE PIERCING EYES AND GOLDEN LOCKS

The thick, grey fog danced around the skeletal trees. Maleficent stood in front of a pitch-black, twinkling tar-like pond. The wind flowed through her rich, velvety curls. An angelic voice appeared from the skeletal trees along with a pair of piercing blue eyes and a head full of golden locks. The figure clasped an embellished, deep purple dagger. Soon enough the golden figure was face-to-face with Maleficent, still singing. She slowly brought the dagger up towards Maleficent's porcelain neck. Her blue eyes glowed and she whispered, "You'll be the one sleeping forever now..." and struck.

Em Nattrass (14)
Studley High School, Studley

SWEET REVENGE

The clock struck nine, silence occurred, loneliness began. The boy stood gobsmacked, fear revealing through his bulging eyes as he saw his mum and dad breathless on the bloody cream carpet. Voices screamed in his spinning head as he wanted and needed sweet, sharp revenge. Applying his knowledge, the boy bravely and miraculously tracked down the sick murderers. *Bang! Bang!* Bullets were dangerously fired. Blood was pouring, covering the tarmacked road in a bright velvety red colour. The brave but unfortunate boy eventually gave his mum and dad's murderers sweet but sharp revenge.

Jacob Miles (14)
Studley High School, Studley

THE FINAL FAIRYTALE FIGHT

Thunder struck! The fight began.

The evil queen flew by Snow White, she moved swiftly. Just as she was passing their eyes met and she could see the shock in Snow's eyes.

She blasted Snow with a beam of her magic and cackled, "You know Snow, after you became queen I thought I failed, but I won't let you win."

The terror on Snow's face formed a smirk, then a laugh.

"Don't be naive..."

The evil queen stopped dead in her tracks. She realised what Snow had done. She felt it. She couldn't win.

Somehow Snow had taken her magic.

Sydney Smith (15)
Studley High School, Studley

TYRONE JENKINS

Tyrone Jenkins, the notorious criminal, was lounging in his mansion. Then blue lights flashed. Sirens bellowed through the acres of land. There was a knock. *Bang!* The door was ploughed down. Voices screamed, "Police!" Tyrone knew exactly what was about to happen. He had made up his mind. Tyrone darted to the staircase wasting no time, he missed three steps at a time. Reaching the roof after a gruesome climb Tyrone relaxed, he thought it was over. He glanced over his shoulder. There stood a figure.
The figure bellowed, "It's over..."

Joe Black (15)
Studley High School, Studley

MR MUNCHER

I was ready! Everyone turned around and looked at me in this alleyway as I screamed down the phone and caused a scene. He gobbled down his curry. Next second a very elderly, dodgy-looking man came to my side and my eyes abruptly opened. Malachi wanted to comfort me with reassuring speak obviously. But no, it was a stern warning. Zachari was alive. The mentally disturbed Zachari was supposed to be dead. I jumped into my blacked-out Cadillac to confront him with a treacherous, life-threatening curry in my hand. I was harmed intensely and burned with my curry bowl.

Johanan Ambrose (15)
Studley High School, Studley

ICICLE

I can finally rest. Little did I know, one of my trustworthy minions would turn on me. But me, I don't care, my heart's as cold as ice. He was a useful minion but I don't need him, I own the world!

The minion turned up unexpectedly and didn't look happy. I said, "What!"

He started talking about how he would be a better leader. By this time, I was snoring with boredom. I awakened as he ended his speech. "This is why I would be bett-"

Bang! That's a shame, he was a good one as well. Back to reading!

James Kirk (14)
Studley High School, Studley

FIRELLA

It was a dark and gloomy morning. Firella was stalking through the village. She had long red hair and red eyes full of hatred. The reason for her hatred was that when she was born she was abandoned at a strict, horrendous orphanage. She was sixteen now and her parents had never visited her. Ever since she was little she knew she was different, mostly because of her name. When she was most angry a fire always started. At first, she thought it was a coincidence however it happened often. She didn't mean to. That didn't stop everyone hating her.

Claudia Smith (15)
Studley High School, Studley

THE AWAKENING

The room seemed to stretch for miles filled with pure screams. We were the chosen ones, they were ones like me. It was damp, moist, humid, and I hated it. Eyes bloodshot red, skin bulbous and pulsating, with spikes stuck in me like jagged peaks. Suddenly a blackout. The lights turned off, one by one. Deactivation was called as the room went dark. I crawled out, my legs like jelly. In the distance, I saw it. Emerging into the light, pupils dilating, stomach wrenching. I saw the only thing left. My punisher, my torturer. No. The only thing left. Death.

Jacob Tagg (14)
Studley High School, Studley

THE TRUTH BEHIND THE FLAMES

Longing for clean air, I scarpered from the flames, pursued by regret, dressed as smoke. I thought what I'd done was justified... until an ash-covered doll rolled wearily to my feet. The ghost of its past owner still etched upon its button face. This was all my fault. Turning to go back, my horrified gaze was met by a merciless stare. The armed forces. "Please let me explain," I pleaded.
It was no use; their minds were a bookstore and my story lay unread on the back shelf. I was only the villain their neglect forced me to become.

Poppy George (14)
Studley High School, Studley

THE RISE OF THE BEAUTY

Scrambling, trying to get up. "Beast!" The forest, pitch-black. "Beast!" he calls again. The beast leaps, ripping Gaston's throat out. The love of Belle's life lies there cold. Was this her plan all along? Belle seemingly full of rage swings around puncturing the beast's heart. Now, this was what she really wanted. Power. The whole castle, just for her. The whole kingdom, under her control. You'd think she would be lonely but Belle didn't care, it was hers, all hers. No longer was there Beauty and the Beast.

Alice Potts (14)
Studley High School, Studley

THE TERMINATOR BEGINS

Once I was a man, once I lived, once I had control. It all stopped one day. A car crash. I was taken. Badly injured, the doctors, they weren't doctors, they said they were. They changed me piece by piece. If I failed a mission they would improve me, change me for tech. Once I escaped, but they caught me. As a punishment, they changed my entire body into an abomination, something I couldn't control. I was conscious in a body that wasn't mine. Something that changed me forever. Something I didn't want to be. I was The Terminator!

Luke Robinson (15)
Studley High School, Studley

THE STORM

It was a dark, lonely day. The water was rough, it was midday but as dark as night. The storm was coming, I was angry. Today was all about the plan. Before I knew it I was rising up, up, further away from the restless ocean. Suddenly I began sprinting towards the land. Screams. Rain poured down, only adding to the excitement I was feeling. Death surrounded me. Silence. The water began to settle, victory overcame me. Thoughts began to circle around me, but swiftly moved on again. The waters were calm again, but the fight had been won, finally.

Charley Freeman (15)
Studley High School, Studley

REVENGE

Sitting lonely by my parents' grave, a tingle rose upon my arm. My arm turned blue, electric. *Powers?* I thought to myself. My very own powers. Revenge could now be achieved. I entered the freezing, dark, desolate warehouse. My breath was cold. My eyes wandered. There I saw him. Unaware of my presence... *Pow!* Electrified. Dead. Stone cold. Revenge was complete.
"I did it for you." Placing a bouquet of flowers at their grave. But, in that moment I'd forgotten those dangerous powers still existed...

Erin McGraham (14)
Studley High School, Studley

I HATE CHRISTMAS

I haven't always hated Christmas you know, I used to love it when I was younger but my parents ruined it for me. It started when I was five, my parents told me that Christmas was a terrible thing and it should have never become a thing. Ever since that day I have never enjoyed Christmas so I take everyone's presents from them so that they won't be able to enjoy Christmas. If it wasn't for my parents I would still enjoy it and wouldn't be stealing presents as soon as Santa delivers them. I really wish I could change.

Sam Todd (14)
Studley High School, Studley

SAVE ME

It was that cold, dull afternoon in the middle of the snowy, stormy hyperthermia-feeling mountain. I had the call, the call that was devastating and hard to take. I was ordered to 'save' someone in freezing breathtaking waters. The order was to 'save' someone and we all knew what 'save' meant. I was stuck in a vicious cycle of killing. I saw the human drowning in the water. I had to record it. I couldn't go through with it. I saved the person and asked them to float in the water to record it. They found out!

George Dickinson (15)
Studley High School, Studley

THE JOKER'S REVENGE

Being rich was nice but being Joker wasn't. As I sat on the pier, I could hear the sirens banging in my ear as I knew they were approaching. Life has no purpose you know, slaying Batman, changed everything. Everyone was so predictable. Why was I a villain? The sunset shone on me, so beautiful and golden. Now I just feel empty inside. I stood by my detonator, thinking where was the bomb. My green lips got bigger, wider with my smile. As their tyres came, I flipped the switch. A bang then silence. The Joker gets away again. Revenge.

Elijah Dutton (15)
Studley High School, Studley

LITTLE RED RIDING HOOD

That day everything turned anti-clockwise as what sounded like a herd of elephants rushed past my window, I glared at that squirming rascal. That evil little girl that everyone calls 'Little Red Riding Hood'. Her coat was red and was probably dyed with blood. Yet I'm framed as the villain. I only gave her a taste of her own medicine. That was the day, as I sat with my plot imprinted in my head, I watched the clock hands do laps. As I feasted on the lifeless body of her grandma the doorbell rang. Haha, sweet, sweet revenge.

Evelyn Messenger (14)
Studley High School, Studley

THE MAN IN BLUE

The night was cold and crisp, I was walking through my field on edge when all of a sudden I was jolted up and nailed to my fence. I tried to break free but my clothes were too strong. The culprit ran as a vicious storm flew across the sky. The lightning crashed and banged in the mist. Thinking about how to get free I suddenly got a rush of pain going through my bones, confused I looked down. "My skin!" I screamed. "It's glowing." I nervously reached out to grab the fence when, *boom!* It became alight.

Michael Cawston (14)
Studley High School, Studley

TWISTED TALE

They screamed at me. "Haha, you freak! No one likes you."
They hit me, they laughed at me. They should fear me, so
they will. They will fear me... I've started now, I can't stop.
I'm hurting them, they are feeling the pain. I feel their pain.
This is good, this is revenge! I was born out of hell for a
reason. They hit me now. They replace me. They're dead!
No! Not again! I feel like me again. I'm going back. I'm
turning back! I have no heart but feel pain. I'm feared by
humans and animals.

Curtis Brooks (14)
Studley High School, Studley

THE INVISIBLE MAN

As the door opened and closed I let the cold draught in. Suddenly I heard loud barks from the dogs. I jumped out the window. Pieces flew everywhere. Sirens were blaring in the distance. I ran with my sack of goodies from house to house. Opening solid vaults and stealing watches, rings and phones. Everything you could think of was dumped in there. It was heavy. I carried it on my back. As I slowly entered through the window I reached into the full sack and pulled out a phone. I returned Katie's lost phone on the side dresser.

Toby Knott
Studley High School, Studley

REVENGE

The sewers are the only place to train alone. Revenge is all I want. First, I had to train myself. Train myself till I'm unstoppable. I won't stop till I'm finished. I almost did it, wipe out the entire human race, but I'm hurt. I need to heal. I'm not going to stop though. They wiped out my species, so I'll wipe out theirs. All on my own too.

I did it, but I regret it. I'm the only living thing left on Planet Earth. I'm so lonely, there's nothing to do. I wish I never did what I did.

Harrison Wheate (14)
Studley High School, Studley

WEIGHT CRUSHER

It's a dark, stormy night, with a horrific gale blowing. I thought about my past, with the reactor incident, my powers, the screams, the terror, Richard. I did it all to survive the disaster. Turns out Richard's alive. I thought I crushed him. I guess the disaster altered his genes as well. I need, I crave revenge. I used my powers to alter my weight to fly to Richard. He was bigger and stronger than before. That didn't matter. I was going to crush him for good, and I did. I won. Finally, I can relax, peacefully.

Benjamin Parry (14)
Studley High School, Studley

THE VICTORIOUS VILLAIN

Finally, I felt victorious. I stood under the dark, clear, starry sky. Pain was all I'd felt for years. It never went away but it was worth it. They all doubted me, now I stood powerful as they begged for mercy. Fire circled around them, leaving them trapped. Isolated. Ready to die. I watched as they got engulfed one by one. Then I felt a presence behind me. It was him, the one I risked it all for. He stood there, his eyes saying it all. Yes, I burned the world down for him and became a deceiving, manipulative villain.

Kevan Kaur (15)
Studley High School, Studley

HOW IT FEELS TO DIE

I sit alone thinking about the people who died because of me. I think about how I wanted to help. How I became my own worst nightmare... My spiralling is rapidly cut short by an aggressive pounding at the door. I rush to answer it. He stands there, once my friend now my rival, looking right at me. "I'm sorry," he whispers.

I look at him, confused until I feel it. The knife plunging into me. I find it somehow poetic that my only love should end my life. At least I will finally know how it feels to die.

Lola Osborne (14)
Studley High School, Studley

SCP-0420

Binary. Binary was all I could see. I could feel the PC taking over my brain. The electrical impulses tingled my body. Suddenly I could feel the force getting weaker. I had my vision back! The PC was lagging and buffering... I thought to celebrate but I had to get away. I was stopped in my tracks: 'Windows update completed' the PC blared. Binary, again! It was taking over my brain at a quicker rate now. I couldn't feel my legs or my arms. I couldn't even hear myself think. Suddenly blackness. Nothing.

Harry Wilkinson (15)
Studley High School, Studley

THE OUTLAW

I never really belonged. My brother betrayed me and took the throne for himself. They believe that a woman cannot rule well, I'll prove them wrong. When my brother was sleeping I snuck into his chamber and stabbed him in the chest. The next morning I woke up to people crowded around the castle. I was confused. *Do they know what I did? What do I do?* I thought I heard screams down the hall so I escaped through the back of the castle. From now on I'll live as an outlaw, walking through the woods.

Casey Barron (14)
Studley High School, Studley

POPPY'S PLAYHOUSE REALITY

Lonely, no one to talk to until this small girl arrived. She seemed very lovely. I stalked her around my abandoned factory for days and days. I think it's time to say hello... I crept out of the dark corner which was my hiding spot and glared down at the small girl. She screamed and hid. I thought we were playing hide-and-seek so I counted to 30 and stomped towards where I thought she was... She wasn't there. I will find her again. I know this factory like the back of my hand. She will never escape...

Tim Vanes (14)
Studley High School, Studley

THE ONE-ARMED FIGURE

Everyone I kill turns into me. I hate this guy called Barron. I want to kill him. "Haha! I will never be like you." Barron mocked me that day. That was a flashback to why I wanted to kill him. Now I find myself outside his house. I am lurking, waiting for him. There he is, goodbye Barron. "Hello there." Oh no!" muttered Barron shocked.

Just like that, I grabbed him with my one arm then killed him. He said he would never be like me. Now I say everyone I kill is like Barron.

Samuel Fowler (14)
Studley High School, Studley

NORMAL

It was a normal morning, at least I thought. I went down my stairs as usual, I got my normal breakfast of normal cereal and normal coffee. I ventured down to my normal comfortable chair. And there it was. Lying there on the normally normal couch in my normal-looking lounge... A body. Not just any body, it was mine... What? Why? How? It didn't make any sense at all. How could a normal man like me be experiencing something so abnormal? My usually normal body was now mangled and rotten. What was going on?

Sarah Lengden (15)
Studley High School, Studley

REDEMPTION

On this day five years ago the villain's parents died. He sought revenge. He saw someone who looked like the person who killed his parents. He chased them, little did he know it was an unknown hero's parent.
After the hero found out, he started to track the villain down. After the hero found him, they charged each other. After a long battle, the hero won but with lots of facial injuries he looked like a zombie. Now known as a local hero he found out that the villain was a serial killer.

Oliver Stanley (15)
Studley High School, Studley

MY DAY OFF

It was a cold stormy morning in Gotham City. I was plotting my ultimate revenge on my arch-enemy, Batman when I realised I needed some time to relax as I had been extremely busy. So I took a slow stroll down to the pet shop to see the new puppies. I played with them all day long. *This is much more fun than revenge,* I thought to myself. It was getting dark so I headed back home and ran a nice warm bubble bath with lots of candles and classical music playing in the background. I was relaxed.

James Humphries (14)
Studley High School, Studley

THE MIND READER

My plan was in motion. I stepped into my office as usual, however today was not usual. I was buzzing, the world would never be quite the same again. I was the first, nobody before me had yet accomplished such a feat. The mind reader. Months of progress and at last it was prepared. The best part? Not one soul was aware, yet, I knew and I was about to know what they knew too. I snapped back down to Earth and sat down at my desk. The time read 9:02am, eight hours until everything changes. Eight hours.

Chloe Kearney (14)
Studley High School, Studley

DAMEON'S TALE

I am doing this for her. Why is this hero trying to stop me? It's a strong, bitter storm. I'm exhausted. Though I need the artefact; I'm going to get it. I wouldn't be here if it weren't for the accident. I long for the day I can see her again. The plane crash crushed her. It crushed my soul. I was a child. Why did it have to be her? Why my mom? It hurts. Never mind that now. Soon she'll be back. If 10% of the population have to perish for me to be complete, so be it.

Ruby Stanway (14)
Studley High School, Studley

HUNTED

My eyes shot open. I pulled a sheet off from over my head and began to sit up. It took me a minute to adjust to my surroundings. I was in a crater of rubble on what seemed to be the top of a building. A screech from a car echoed down below. I sprung from the ground, my aching limbs hung heavily. I dragged myself to the edge of the roof, my eyes widened as an immense number of policemen were shouting below. I closed my eyes and as soon as I did, the building next to me collapsed.

Evie Troth (15)
Studley High School, Studley

A DAY

Me, the king of the ocean. My mouth was full of daggers; ready to kill and catch my next victim. I was hungry. People all around me, water splashing above, shrieking and screaming filled my ears. People were happy; enjoying themselves. Every move was planned out, ready to pounce. Doubt started to engulf me, I was questioning myself. This would always happen. Worry. Fear. *Should I really do this now? Kill all these innocent people? Everyone needs to eat though, right?*

Ellie Blizzard (14)
Studley High School, Studley

MY BIGGEST MISTAKE

How could she do this to me? I thought she loved me. I should never have trusted her... It was a normal Wednesday evening. I was working late on a patient again when all of a sudden I let the voice get ahold of me. I allowed myself to commit its evil plan. There she was. My patient lying dead on the table. Blood leaking everywhere, her baby screaming in the background. What had I done? Being the quick-witted midwife I was I thought of a plan and I thought of it quickly...

Faith Sheen (15)
Studley High School, Studley

FAULT NOT MINE

Isolated, not by choice but by manipulation. They're always there 24/7, I can't escape their menacing hands, they grasp me and control me. Trying to escape has led to me falling into this dark hole. I'm sorry to those I've hurt, it wasn't me, it was him. I hope you can tell I can't control my behaviour. I just want to be normal. As you can see the biggest villain of all lives inside my head. It was my hands that murdered but in no way was it me.

Sophie Tolley (14)
Studley High School, Studley

THE ROBOTS

Growing up I never had friends. So instead of friends I created robots and to get my revenge I created five killer robots... Today is the day I get my revenge on the world. Today I am going to release the robots on the world... They have now been released, but suddenly, *bam!* I get hit in the face by them so they now have betrayed me and are going to kill me and help the world by destroying all the villains on the Earth!

Lewis Sproston (14)
Studley High School, Studley

THE END OF IT

My plan was in motion. I strode into the city with my army. Lion led the way, demolishing everyone in his path. Mayhem rushed through the city. Screams suffocated the air. This is what I'd been waiting for. It was time for revenge. Payback for what they did to us. We patrolled through the streets leaving a trail of blood. We took no prisoners. All mankind would be gone soon. Gone forever! I did it to survive... For us to survive.

Alyssa Blackford (15)
Studley High School, Studley

THE LONER

He stood still, memories flooded his mind. The torture he was given. Hades laughed and screamed as his parents spun him around. If only it was real. But he was just there. Alone. Dragging his feet along the stone floor, his footsteps echoed. 'The weirdo' and 'The loner' he was called. Well, he did wear roughed-up rags with flaming blue hair. But he didn't deserve it. No one does.

Amie Jeff (15)
Studley High School, Studley

VILLAINOUS

At last, Lila was gaining her revenge, not just on her sister but on the two monstrosities that defeated Andre. All Andre wanted was the two most omnipotent 'things' that gave these heroes their powers. However, it wasn't that easy. All that Lila could do was keep walking, absorbing more energy into her glittering gold heels.

Earlier that day, Lila's manipulative and spoiled sister, Chloe, had commanded her to push Maria down the elevated, levitating staircase. She felt this urge, waiting for revenge. And because she could not do it, a black and dark magenta butterfly seeped into her sneakers.

Alfie Stone (16)
Tamworth Enterprise College, Belgrave

WHAT HAVE YOU DONE?

She frowned.

"What have you done?"

She spoke as she sighed in despair, "I haven't done anything."

I plastered a clueless expression on my face. The confusion drained out of her. It didn't work. The decapitated remains she had covered returned to her memory. She perceived the truth, eyes widened. I could see the rage building up. The regular drone of cars rushing past, built up in my head, causing my thoughts to feel so overwhelming. I felt I could hear everything and my heart was pounding out of my chest. I'd created this twisted truth, but I'd ruined it.

Holly Roughton (13)
Tamworth Enterprise College, Belgrave

THE SHADY FOREST

One dark, gloomy night a man cackled with a menacing smile on his distorted face. But it wasn't just the villain that was there because there were far more sinister voices that echoed throughout the shady forest. The voices cried out for help while groaning for salvation. However, only a handful of people were tricked by this real villain. It all happened like this... Four people wandered mindlessly into the forest but they heard voices so they followed the voices but were grabbed by a shadowy figure and dragged by brute strength from the darkness. Hopefully they'll return.

Jensen-John Madden (11)
Tamworth Enterprise College, Belgrave

THEY DIDN'T DESERVE THIS

My brain numb from it, this day has turned away from the squelching sun to my mind going blank. It confused me, though the red sauce that entranced this mind-melting day, still reminiscent. Those errors in my life, the long drawn-out days of winter to the nights of summer, my mind unable to think, the everlasting thought that maybe what I did was wrong, that they didn't deserve this. As the day comes to a close so does the pulsation of his heart in my hand, the sauce no longer clenching my warmness but covering me in extreme heat...

Luke Downward (14)
Tamworth Enterprise College, Belgrave

THE REAL HERO

As those people cheered to their hero I was stuck in the dark wondering when it was my turn to shine. I've done good things for those people, yet they praise someone who knocked me down. I was raised to be like this. I cannot help it, but since they're begging, I will show them my dark side. I will set things on fire, burn down the 'hero's' fame. I will get it all for free now. I will hunt down the ones who seek the hero. I will become the greatest. He shouldn't have the fame that I deserve!

Erin Royston (14)

Tamworth Enterprise College, Belgrave

SPECIAL MISSION

I woke up after a rough sleep. Running from police every two minutes was exhausting. Anyways, I skipped over to my lair and got my new suit on. I walked over to the mission board and... today would be the best... Blowing up the whole city of Birmingham. At this point, I was all ready to go so I headed (in my fancy car) to Birmingham fully equipped. I first cleared a couple of holes underground and filled them up with my specially made bombs and ran away. My timer counted down, 3, 2, 1... Birmingham was in bits.

Grace Hollyoak (12)

Tamworth Enterprise College, Belgrave

THE BROKEN MAN IN THE BOMB

As the building fell, Wilbur walked from the door crying. "It's done, now you can rest," he said while getting into his Mustang and driving away, his curly brown hair blowing in the wind. You may think he's a villain, but let's go back a bit. Wilbur was happy, he had a son, Henry, and a wife, Sally.
"Daddy, Daddy, look I made you something."
Henry gave his father a small bracelet. Then, *bang!* A gunshot echoed through the house. Sally and Henry dropped dead.
Not all villains are bad guys, some are just broken. Just like poor Wilbur.

Emma Wood (13)
The Corbet School Technology College, Baschurch

THE HAUNTING OF HIM

Rain hammered against the glass windowpanes and the wind shrieked outside whilst I roamed the empty hallway. I knew he was here and I was eager to get my revenge... My tale ended tragically. I was too intelligent for my time which was my ruin. I detested my husband and expressed it constantly. I read forbidden books and practised with herbs to his distaste. Unfortunately, having practised these arts, it was only a matter of time before I was arrested and accused of witchcraft. Nobody helped me and I was sent to a decaying, lifeless castle where heartbroken I died.

Emily Staniforth (13)

The Corbet School Technology College, Baschurch

RAPUNZEL

Lifting her bike up from the bike stand, Mother Gothel waved goodbye to Hilda as she walked past. She had joined the knitting club two years ago after Rapunzel had escaped from the tower with the prince, leaving her all alone. She rode home, her head fuelled with thoughts of Rapunzel (as always). Despite Rapunzel leaving over two years ago, Mother Gothel still carried on thinking of her and looking for her on a daily basis. She got home and went straight to her room. The room was filled with maps, newspaper articles and all possibilities for getting Rapunzel back.

Bethany Inns (13)
The Corbet School Technology College, Baschurch

I JUST WANT TO MAKE FRIENDS

I heard footsteps coming. Yay! My chance to make some real friends, not just an antique wardrobe. I stepped out the door as they came round the corner. "Ghost!" they screamed. They stood there, paralysed in shock. Then they turned and ran. I sprinted after them, confused and startled. All I wanted was to not be lonely. Why were they scared? I'm a good ghost, not mean. I did nothing wrong. I tried to shout them, tell them what I wanted, but all I said was, "Boo!" They started running faster. All I wanted to do was make some friends!

Bethany Williams (13)
The Corbet School Technology College, Baschurch

THE LONE GHOST

Vengeful from last Halloween, a spectre was roaming the forest. His rage carried him to a house in which he found two children. He found them so repugnant, he seized them by their necks and slammed the children to the wall. The children, in utter disbelief, didn't speak. The spectre released the children, but before they could escape, he retrieved an axe from his skull and slaughtered the children one by one. Their limp bodies fell cold on the floor. Feeling accomplished, he rested in the main hall, but all of a sudden, he heard a knock on the door...

Rory Strang (12)
The Corbet School Technology College, Baschurch

SCARS

Once upon a time, about 70 years ago, a man lived, an old man 50 or so. He lived in a horrible decaying, inexplicable, repugnant smelling house. The smell was due to the dozens of rotting, decomposing bodies. He obviously killed them and stored them in this house isolated from all sanity. His face told the stories of his victims' deaths, it showed the efforts to stay alive. Gun wounds, knife scratches and everything in-between. You could take this man to court and know the full story with just a quick glance of his torturing and tormenting face.

Ella Maybin (12)
The Corbet School Technology College, Baschurch

INSIDE MY HEAD

I could feel the blood rushing to my cheek, the cold, unwavering eyes of my brother drilling into my own, his mouth rising into a smirk. "You okay Cato?"
I didn't have to look to know everyone in the training room was watching, and as much as I wanted to attack, fight back, I stood and walked out; no reaction. Instead, I walked home and prepared for the reaping. In other districts they saw the Hunger Games as torture, but here in Two we saw it as an exciting opportunity to bring pride to our districts, our families and ourselves!

Emma Weir (12)
The Corbet School Technology College, Baschurch

DEFEATED

So here I lie, in the rubble of my 'lair', my home. Defeated. I never wanted to be the bad guy, I dreamt about saving the day. That's gone out the window. I used to gaze up at the stars before bed, picturing myself flying across the city, stopping villains as my cape fluttered in the wind. I got bullied at school quite a lot by the 'heroes'. The amazing, heroic, superheroes. I never fitted in anywhere and tended to stay quiet. That's who the bullies aim for. They ruined me. I quietly plotted my revenge. But I was defeated.

Harry Ninnis (12)
The Corbet School Technology College, Baschurch

NEVER TURN YOUR BACK

I stepped onto the marshy, clumpy soil of a grave. I looked up to see black then ruins, ravens squawking as they saw me. My cloak was violently swaying behind me. As I walked forward onto the irregular patchy grass, the overwhelming eeriness hit me; apart from the ravens it was only moonlight and wind that surrounded me. Then icy fingers grabbed my arm. I screamed, then the lights of the half-ruined castle lit up. Who was this holding my arm? I heard the faint baying of wolves closing in around me. I had to escape from this horrid place.

Bea Lewis (12)
The Corbet School Technology College, Baschurch

HEART OF A QUEEN

You all know the story. My sister lied, I hit my head, became evil, blah blah blah. But I'm not the real monster. The real villain of Wonderland is my sister. Ever wonder why I spared Alice? It was to protect her from the evil witch. But no, I'm the evil, angry one, no one believed me. The Jabberwocky was my best chance to free Wonderland from her pale curse. Poor Alice was too late to realise, Wonderland isn't really wonderful, it's a place built on war and power. My humble people died at the hands of the White Queen.

Kim Gibbons (12)

The Corbet School Technology College, Baschurch

THE DESPERATE SCREAM

Giggles, laughter became noticeable instead of hearing the howls of the wind creeping through the gaps of the shattered window which completely filled my ears. In the distance, as the old lights of the narrow hallways flickered, the classical phone rang. The cries of laughter stopped. My breathing got quicker. I began walking towards the end door. A desperate scream broke the silence. The lights went dark. I could hear my heart pounding. My legs shaking, my spine went as cold as ice. I froze as I slowly and carefully turned to see...

Lily Poston (13)
The Corbet School Technology College, Baschurch

HOW THE GRIM REAPER CAME TO BE

I stood and stared. The loss of a pet is extremely hard to cope with, especially when it's one you've had for years. From that day on, I wanted to experiment on anything deceased so I could create something to revive my pet. People saw me as an enemy, taking their loved ones away from them, just like the universe took mine away. I would spend hours each day figuring out a solution to bring my rabbit back, when it happened. The corpse rose up slowly and my rabbit was back. People still hate me because I'm the Grim Reaper.

Jack Munn (12)
The Corbet School Technology College, Baschurch

A DULL BOY

My Wendy, I wish only for our shadows to stand side by side, to simply connect our words under the moonlight. You are every thought, every feeling, every snowflake melting outside and I've been static for too long. I have found that while I roam these floors with the same ugly carpet I have come to hate endlessly, my mind emptily follows my feet, entwining with woe himself. Have I flown too close to the sun? Become one with Icarus himself? For now I will lift my axe, bury my thoughts and become all work, no play. A dull boy.

Lily Ford (12)
The Corbet School Technology College, Baschurch

THE BLACK BRICK ROAD

I said to the Wicked Witch of the West, "They're gone, I got rid of them and the road is replaced."
Yes, I did kill the tin man, the lion and the scarecrow and yes, I replaced the yellow brick road with the black brick road. As soon as Dorothy left, I thought being kind was boring. The road needed a twist with colour as black as a sad soul. I, the Good Witch of the North committed murder. The bulging black bricks were slotted into place and the three people/animals were killed by a knife through the heart.

Izzy Cartwright (12)
The Corbet School Technology College, Baschurch

MIDNIGHT IN THE FOREST

It all started at midnight in the house in the forest. A mysterious man was working in a lab, he looked very concentrated. He opened a fridge and a cloud of smoke came to his face. He pulled out an arm, he started putting it together and a weird beast arose and grabbed the lights in the room. It trashed the place. It ran outside and went on a killing rampage and the mysterious man went after him. He caught up eventually and stabbed the beast's heart. He fell dead upon the spot and the mysterious man sighed with relief.

Sophie Gibbs (12)
The Corbet School Technology College, Baschurch

THE QUEEN OF HEARTS

The Queen of Hearts was the only child until the White Queen came along. She grew more jealous by the day as the White Queen got all of the attention. She realised that her head began to grow and grow even more every week. Their mother entered them both in a beauty contest like she did every year.

It was the final result and it was just the Queen of Hearts and the White Queen left. The White Queen won. The Queen of Hearts stormed off, her head grew so big the beautifully decorated headband snapped off into pieces.

Maddy Carter (12)
The Corbet School Technology College, Baschurch

THE EVIL QUEEN KILLED SNOW WHITE

I was sick and tired of her being the centre of attention so I cast a spell upon her. The spell would become effective on the day of her wedding. Today was that day, the day where she would no longer be the most beautiful. I grew impatient until she finally said those two necessary words 'I do'. At that moment her face grew thin and wrinkly and lost all its colour, the same as her hair. I thought it would stop there however she fell to the ground. Snow screamed in pain until she couldn't. She had died.

Lily Thomas (12)
The Corbet School Technology College, Baschurch

JAFAR'S STORY

I've always been second best. Been like that for years now. First with my idiotic brother and then the sultan. I've had it. Is it too much to ask to be best at something for once? My older brother, always so perfect, so great, but I showed him. I control him now and I'm most powerful. Before this I lived in constant fear. As soon as it was done I regretted it. His power grew, he became strong but I showed him and now he's forever encased in brass, trapped forever in the diamond in the rock...

Megan Lawson (12)
The Corbet School Technology College, Baschurch

INSIDE MY HEAD (MALEFICENT)

My eyes slowly opened, felt exposed. I'd never felt this before. What had happened? I crumbled to the ground. My wings had gone! My glee had been absorbed by my despair. *Why?* I thought. I became more drained and evil as time went on. In the course of time news came to me the king was having a baby. I rushed to the castle and when I glanced at him bad memories came flashing back. I was angry and cursed the baby. This baby brought joy back to my life, it was like a flower was growing inside of me.

Lola-Sophia Hardie (12)

The Corbet School Technology College, Baschurch

COTTON CANDY KILLER

I didn't mean to, honest I didn't (well that's a lie but he doesn't need to know that). Well, you are probably wondering where I just am, I am in jail. I am just going to put it out there, I am a murderer. Every murderer has a back story and here is mine... My father left me when I was eight at a bus stop with only a piece of cotton candy. I was hurt, ill and then I killed. Killed anyone who came near my cotton candy shop. Why let the parents leave when I could just kill...

Emily Whitmore (12)
The Corbet School Technology College, Baschurch

ICE KING

If love could cure an endless feeling of solidarity, wouldn't you take any measure to secure it? Living your life in a barren cave with only penguins for company can twist a poor mentality for anyone. Though kidnapping princesses isn't the most suitable strategy he obviously felt pressured that it was his only option to motivate contact. Such conditions for being raised could forge poor social skills which further add to his credibility. The power of isolation is a great curse.

James Nicoll (13)
The Corbet School Technology College, Baschurch

IN THE CAVE

I came across a cave and as soon as I entered, the smell hit me like a tsunami. I saw crows and vultures pecking at a not long-dead body. I walked further in to see a house, but all the lights were on. I steadily walked towards it. Then a smell hit me, rotting, it was so repugnant. I had to run past it holding my nose. The smells were so inexplicable and vile my eyes started watering. In an instant an eyeless man jumped out of a dark corner, his clothing dirty and chased me out.

Chloe Walsh (12)
The Corbet School Technology College, Baschurch

BIG SNEEZY WOLF

My morning went great until my mum kicked me out my house. I was lonely. Then I saw a pig, building a house made out of straw. I went to say hi but then I sneezed. As I sneezed I blew down the house. I was so sorry but he ran away. Then again I saw a house made of wood. I went to see if I could live with him but my cold grew to make me sneeze. The house fell down and they ran! Then a brick house stood out, as I walked, I got trapped!

Isabel Osborne (12)
The Corbet School Technology College, Baschurch

THE DROIDS

The screen went blue, flashing lines of white text.
Suddenly the voice of the AI shouted, "Systems online, droid production initialised."
I furiously typed into the command box: 'Cancel droid production.exe'.
The voice yelled, "Silence, Meat."
The door behind me opened. Six C1 droids started firing their energy weapons. I ran behind a server wall. The mechanical force of the AI shouted, "You cannot hide Meat." The droid got a stun grenade out. It landed at my feet, detonating immediately. I felt the cold metallic hand grasp me, dragging me along the smoky floor of the facility. I passed out.

Max Brealey (12)
The Hamble School, Hamble

THE FERRY BOATMAN'S REAL THOUGHTS

The underworld. Many mere mortals try not to think about death - especially what comes after. But without death, I'd be nothing. For I'm the ferry boatman. Without me, there'd be no afterlife! Souls would be stuck forever, never able to move on. Although condemned souls would think themselves lucky. Not a day goes by that I don't hear the agonised screaming of tortured ghosts. I've learnt to enjoy their cries - Hades knows what I would become if not. Constantly rowing my boat, I know that even I can never leave. Here in the dark, we are all stuck for eternity.

Kate Rowlands (12)
The Hamble School, Hamble

HALF-BLOOD FREAK

I was on the ground. "Half-blood freak!" Peter said. My arm was bleeding, I could feel the tears.

"Look, she's crying and what name is Dolores!" laughed Maddie.

Everyone was mocking me. I ran and ran. I didn't know where to hide. All of a sudden a room of requirement opened into a room of pink with puppies and kittens. That's when I knew I had to straighten kids for the next generation. They call me weird but the reason I have pictures of dogs and cats, let's just say they were the cute animals that died 15 years ago...

Sophie O'Brien (11)
The Hamble School, Hamble

DEATH'S END

I am Death. The greatest fear to every human on Earth. My tale is how I reached the heavens, trying desperately to fix the past, cure my curse. Those in the skies had punished me with the task of taking unfortunate souls to their doom. I despise my job, sharing a plague of misery everywhere I go. I attempted to fly, soaring up into the skies, black-feathered wings spread wide. Finally, I reached the clouds, circling above thousands of shimmering figures - angels. Suddenly a warm sense of peace filled me. Feeling incredible my wings melted and I fell. Free.

Beth Rowlands (12)
The Hamble School, Hamble

BLOOD IS THICKER THAN WATER

Ever heard of a horned beast named Maleficent? That would be me, known as the capturer and villain of Sleeping Beauty or Aurora. Although you don't know it all... Aurora, daughter of Stefan and Leah, that's a lie... The girl belongs to me, or at least in the real world. In stories, no, she is a royal child. Even when my blood matches hers they deny it. They bring this point up... Why did you try to kill her? I simply put her to sleep to scare her parents. Then I brought her back. Now you people should believe my word.

Isobel O'Brien (11)

The Hamble School, Hamble

FALLEN

For months I was tortured, abused and hurt. Not only physically but mentally. My loved ones were threatened, I was put through agonising pain. I had no choice but to comply. They made me hurt the innocent, destroy beautiful homes and landscapes. I didn't want to do this. The way people looked at me was the thing I hated. The fear in their eyes, the strain in their screams, it wounded me. They now see me how I used to see myself. I used to live in the shadows, but now I am in living hell. Please help me!

Daisie Phelps (14)
The Hamble School, Hamble